Sunday Dinner

at

Silly Yaya's

Story and Illustrations by
Violet Favero

This book is dedicated to my parents;

my Mother, who taught me to care

for and feed the world and

my Father, the gentlest man I know,

who makes the best bread,

pizza and meatballs

on this earth.

A special thank you to my son,

Matthew Favero for your graphic

editing and illustration advisement

and to Barbara Leek for your

outstanding editing and patience.

ISBN-10: 1517127777

ISBN-13: 978-1517127770

Illustrations rendered with colored pencil and ink.

Printed by CreateSpace, An Amazon.com Company

First Printing 2016

Our family eats dinner
together once a week.

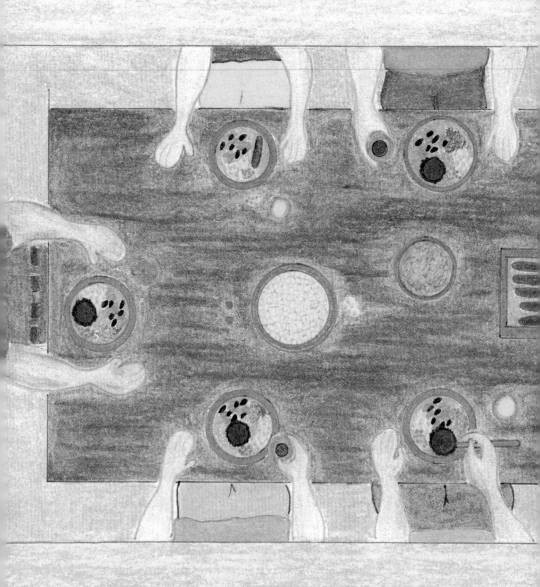

It's a tradition and a treat.

It even has its own day
of the week. It's called Sunday
Dinner at Silly Yaya's.

"So let's look at the menu board
to see what we'll eat!"

And the little one's are always
at Yaya's feet.

Lamb,
Ham &
Spam

Snow
Peas,
Feta
Cheese
& Grape
Leaves

Sweets,
Treats
& Beets

Everyone is so busy with soccer and dance, Sundays are the only time we have a chance.

We do family dinner every
Sunday you see.
Hosted by Bobbis and
cooking by me.

Because he's the honoree,
Papoo sits on this end you see

and on other end, it's
Bobbis and me.

When we sit down to eat,
we talk about this
and we talk about that.
The first to go is usually Matt.

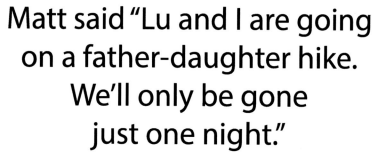

Matt said "Lu and I are going
on a father-daughter hike.
We'll only be gone
just one night."

Bobbis told that silly joke
one more time.
As usual, it did not rhyme.

Unkie Munkie,
who lives at the zoo,
told us he just got
his first kangaroo.

Lisa who walked over in her bare feet,
told Kim to get out of her seat.

Kim who always wants dessert first,
told us she had a cupcake in her purse!

Wendy who grooms dogs all day,
told a story about the one
that tried to get away.

With hardly any hair on his head,
Papoo bakes his famous bread.

Mia said, "I can confirm,
I really am a bookworm!"

Call or text if you're going to come.
So I can make enough for your
tummy to say "yum, yum, yum!"

I'll shop till I drop,

then I'll cook and
chop, chop, chop.

So many come to Silly Yaya's
to eat, cars are parked
up and down the street,
Don't come late,
you may not get a plate!

So now that everyone is here
and dinner is almost ready,
the house is filled with laughter,
love and family cheer.

Now, Lu the youngest rings
the dinner bell,
to tell everyone dinner
is ready and oh
what a great smell!

They've eaten so quick,
the dinner was over
lickety split!

Now that we've eaten,
cleaned and cleared,
it's time to put that
dessert right here.

"Maybe it's cake?
Maybe it's pie?
Or whipped cream on ice cream,"
the little one's cry!

Now that everyone is full of sweets, it's time to go home and get ready for the new week.

Until next week again when we meet,
Silly Yaya gives you hugs and kisses
and all her best wishes.

Even if you can't get together
once a week to eat,
being together with family
is always a treat.

The most important
thing of all,
love your family,
be it big or small!

Silly Yaya's Greek Vinaigrette

1/3 Cup of Olive Oil

3 Tab Red Wine Vinegar

2 Tab Lemon Juice

1/2 Teas Oregano

1 Teas Sugar

1/4 Teas Black Pepper

1 Clove Finely Minced Garlic

Add all ingredients to a cruet or jar and shake to mix well. Store in the refrigerator for up to two weeks.